P9-AGR-460

Adapted by **Sheila Sweeny Higginson**
Based on the episode written by **Joe Ansolabehere**
for the series created by **Sascha Paladino**

ABDOPUBLISHING.COM

Reinforced library bound edition published in 2019 by Spotlight, a division of ABDO, PO Box 398166, Minneapolis, Minnesota 55439. Spotlight produces high-quality reinforced library bound editions for schools and libraries. Published by agreement with Disney Press, an imprint of Disney Book Group.

Printed in the United States of America, North Mankato, Minnesota.
042018 092018

New York • Los Angeles

THIS BOOK CONTAINS RECYCLED MATERIALS

Library of Congress Control Number: 2017961284

Publisher's Cataloging in Publication Data

Names: Higginson, Sheila Sweeny, author. | Ansolabehere, Joe, author. | Disney Storybook Art Team, illustrator.
Title: Miles From Tomorrowland: How I saved my summer vacation / by Sheila Sweeny Higginson and Joe Ansolabehere; illustrated by Disney Storybook Art Team.
Description: Minneapolis, MN : Spotlight, 2019 | Series: World of reading level 1
Summary: Miles and Loretta team up with alien friends to discover the secret to releasing the planet's water supply and save their summer vacation.
Identifiers: ISBN 9781532141928 (lib. bdg.)
Subjects: LCSH: Miles from Tomorrowland (Television program)--Juvenile fiction. | Family vacations--Juvenile fiction. | Space--Juvenile fiction. | Aquifers--Juvenile fiction. | Readers (Primary)--Juvenile fiction.
Classification: DDC [E]--dc23

Spotlight
A Division of ABDO
abdopublishing.com

Miles is all set for a summer vacation.
He has his beach ball.
He has his swimsuit.

"Orange sands, blue seas," Miles says. "This is going to be our best vacation ever!"

Dad flies the spaceship.
“Here we are, kids!” Mom says.
It is the planet Alarbus!

The Callistos check into the resort.
“Weird,” says Loretta.
“We’re the only family here.”

Miles does not care.
The gift shop is full of blastastic rocks.
He buys one for his collection.

The Callistos are ready to hit the beach.
“Where’s the water?” Miles asks.
He cannot surf in the sand!

Ruggles the Robot is in charge
of activities.
The tour of the alien ruins is leaving.
Miles and Loretta are in!

"Have a good time, kiddos," Dad says. "We'll stay here and relax."

SPACETASTIC FACT:
Mars is nicknamed the Red Planet, because it's made mostly of metals and reddish-orange rock.

Miles, Loretta, and Merc follow Ruggles. "Here are the beautiful blue oceans of Alarbus," Ruggles says.

"Oops," says Ruggles. "That was the old tour."

SPACETASTIC FACT:
The Atacama Desert in Chile is the driest place in the world.

"What happened to the oceans?" Miles asks.

SPACETASTIC FACT:
About 71 percent of the earth is covered by water. Most of that is ocean water.

“We don’t know,” Ruggles says.
“The water dried up after we got here.”

They get to the alien ruins.
"Kind of dinky, don't you think?"
Miles says.

SPACETASTIC FACT:
Most Egyptian pyramids were built
to be tombs for pharaohs.

Miles grabs the top of a ruin.
The floor opens up.
WHOA!
They all slip down a rocky slide.

"What is this place?" Miles asks.
"I think we're inside the ruins,"
Loretta says.

Loretta holds up her BraceLex.
It reads the writing on the wall.
Beware all who enter here.

Miles sees two strange shadows.
"Stay back, sand monsters!" he yells.

“We’re not sand monsters,” one creature says. “We’re sand kids! I’m Melvin. This is my sister Melinda.”

Melvin and Melinda are lost, too.
They all need to find a way out.

Melinda reads the writing on the wall. "The ancient builders could turn the water on and off," she says.

The builders used a key to control the water.
The key looks like the rock Miles got in the gift shop!

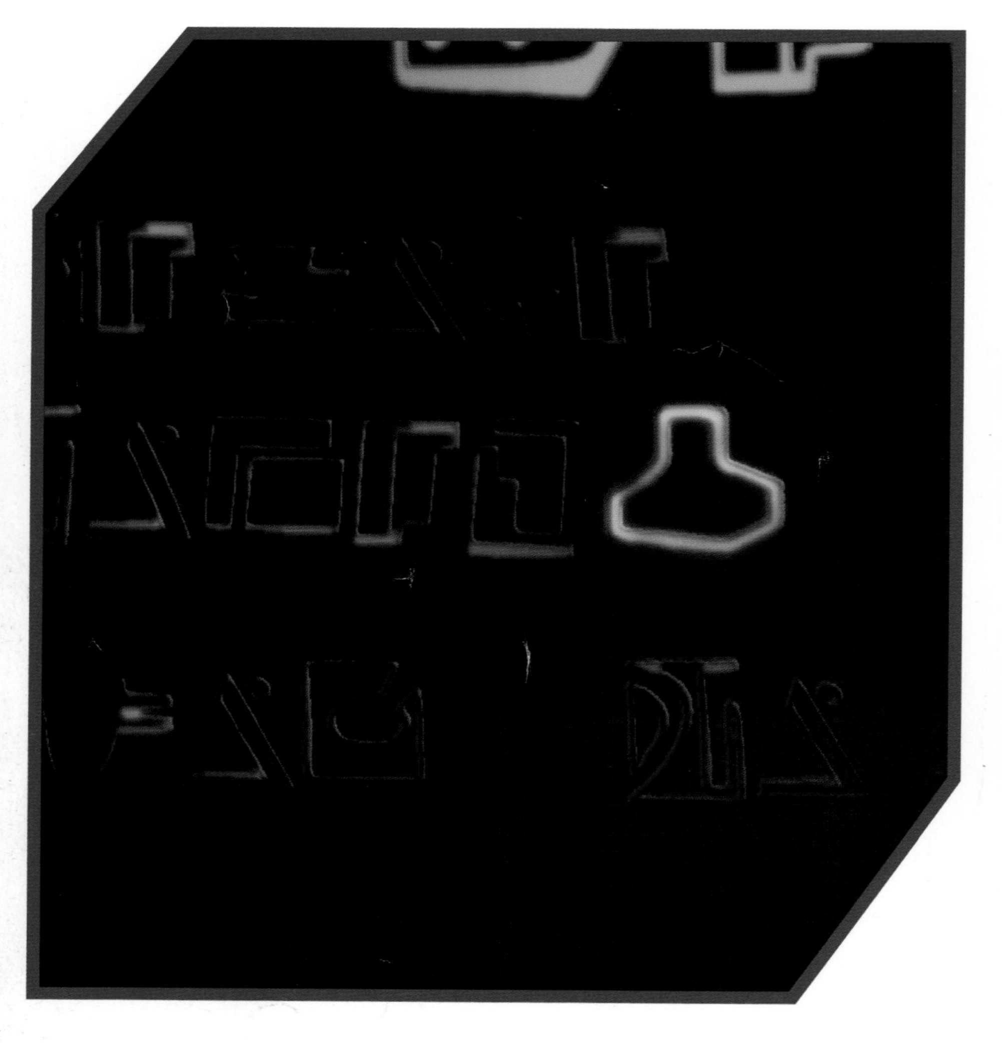

Miles grabs his rock.
He places it in the lock.
It fits!

A column lights up.

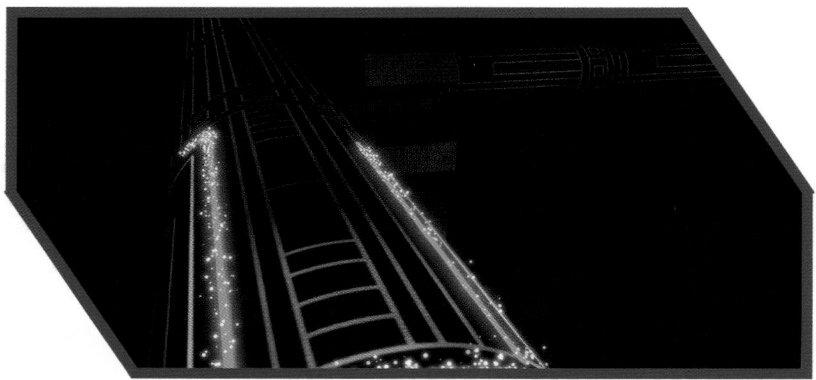

Gears begin to turn.

Water starts to flow.

"I think we found the ocean!"
Miles says.
"And here it comes!" Loretta yells.
"Run!" They climb a ladder to safety.

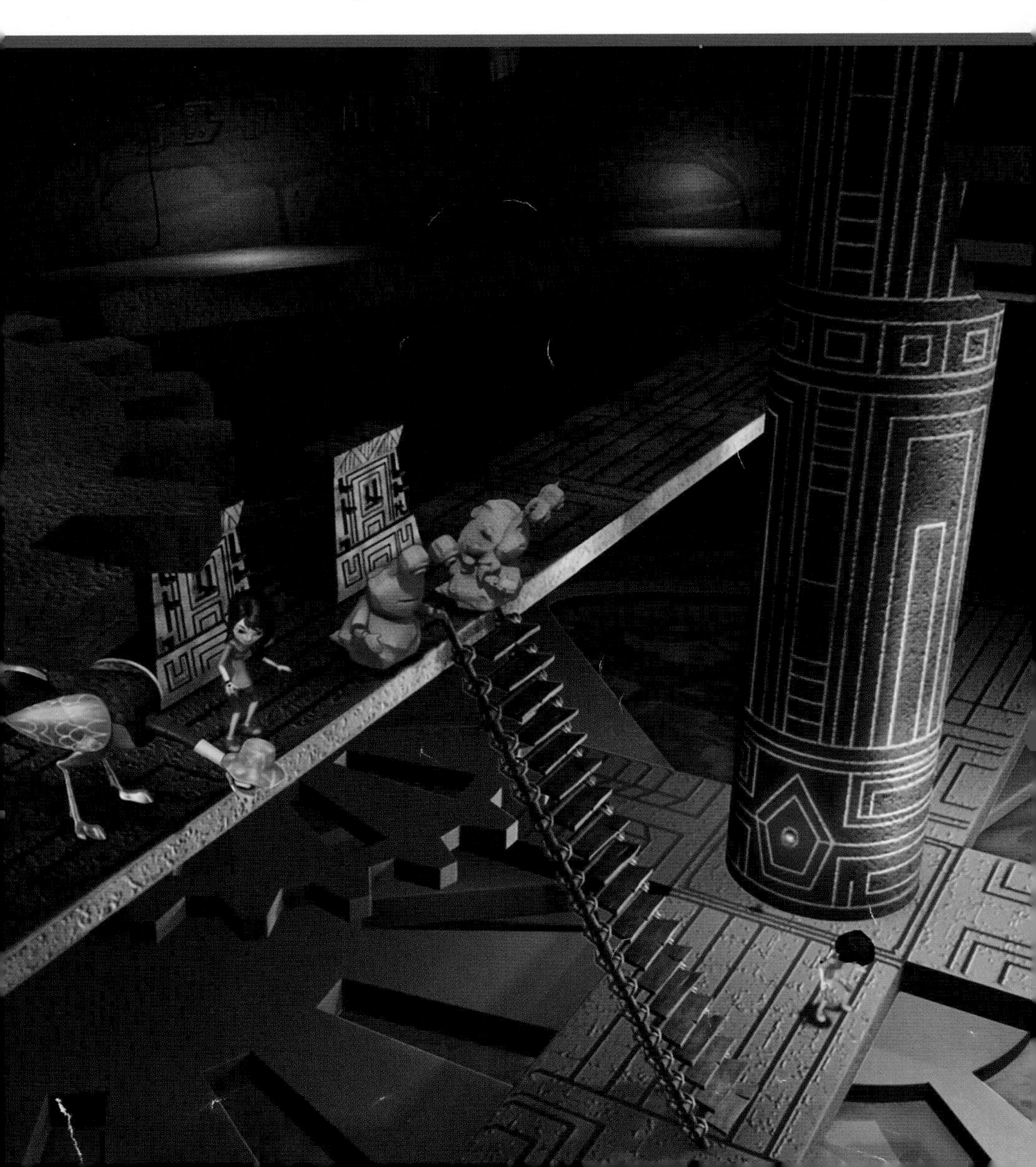

"I wish we had a boat," says Loretta.
Miles sees a wooden door.
He launches his laserang at the door.

The door falls into the water.
Now it's a raft!
"Here's our ride!" Miles says.

The raft goes over a waterfall.
"Hold on tight!" Loretta yells.
They ride the raft to the beach.

“Miles! Loretta!” Mom cries.
“Are you okay?” Dad asks.
“We’re superstellar!” Miles says.

Loretta explains everything.
The builders made a system to control the water.
The rocks were keys.
The robots turned it off when they collected all the rocks.

Miles, Loretta, and Merc help return all the rocks.
Soon Alarbus looks like a vacation planet again.

SPACETASTIC FACT:
The use of water to generate electricity—called hydroelectricity—began in the late nineteenth century.

“I LOVE ALARBUS!” Miles cheers.
And thanks to Miles and his family,
so does everyone else!